The Flower Princess

and other princess stories

Compiled by Tig Thomas

Miles
Kelly

First published in 2013 by Miles Kelly Publishing Ltd
Harding's Barn, Bardfield End Green, Thaxted, Essex, CM6 3PX, UK

This edition printed 2014

4 6 8 10 9 7 5 3

Publishing Director Belinda Gallagher
Creative Director Jo Cowan
Editorial Director Rosie Neave
Senior Editor Claire Philip
Senior Designer Joe Jones
Production Manager Elizabeth Collins
Reprographics Stephan Davis, Jennifer Cozens, Thom Allaway
Assets Lorraine King

ISBN 978-1-78209-211-7

Printed in China

British Library Cataloguing-in-Publication Data
A catalogue record for this book is available from the British Library

ACKNOWLEDGEMENTS

The publishers would like to thank the following artists who have contributed to this book:
Marcin Piwowarski, Kirsten Wilson, Mélanie Florian (inc. cover), Smiljana Coh

All other artwork from the Miles Kelly Artwork Bank

The publishers would like to thank the following sources for the use of their photographs:
Cover frame: Karina Bakalyan/Shutterstock.com
Inside frame: asmjp/Shutterstock.com

Made with paper from a sustainable forest

www.mileskelly.net   info@mileskelly.net

Contents

The Princess Emily

A retelling of **The Knight's Tale**
by Geoffrey Chaucer

ANY YEARS AGO, there lived a noble king called Theseus, with his wife Hippolyta, the queen of the Amazons, and her niece, Princess Emily. Emily was as lovely as a pure white lily upon its stalk of delicate green.

On the first day of May, she awoke early and went to gather flowers and sing about the joys of the morning. She had never looked more lovely, with her hands full of flower blossoms and the sun shining on her

beautiful blonde hair.

It just so happened that King Theseus had two knights in his prison. They had been captured fighting against him. Their names were Palamon and Arcite and they were best friends.

On this day, Palamon heard Emily singing and went to look out of the dark window from which he could catch a glimpse of the gardens. He gasped and cried, "A goddess!

Surely she must be a goddess! Maybe even Venus, the goddess of love herself." And in that moment Palamon's heart belonged to Emily forever.

Arcite leapt up and looked out of the window for himself.

"That's no goddess!" he cried, "but the most beautiful human the gods have ever made. I shall love her all my life."

"But Arcite," cried Palamon, "I saw her and fell in love with her first. Surely you will respect that?"

"You didn't even know she was a human," said Arcite. "I fell in love with a girl — you only worshipped a goddess."

In just one moment their friendship was finished forever. Each hoped to win Emily one day, and neither would speak to the other again. Their only joy came from watching Emily walk in the gardens whilst loving her from afar.

Many months later, Arcite's ransom was paid, and King Theseus released him back to his home country of Thebes. There he pined away dreaming only of the beautiful Emily. His face grew pale and his body lost its strength. Then he had an idea.

'No one would know me now,' he thought. 'I shall return to the court of King Theseus as a servant.'

This he did, becoming a squire of King Theseus. His joy was in spending time near Emily, bringing logs in for her fire, watching her dance, sing or talk but never daring to speak to her directly.

After seven long years in prison, Palamon finally escaped. He went to the forest, and one day while he was hiding there, Arcite came riding through on his horse. It was May Day once more, and he had come to gather a woodland garland for Emily's rooms. As he gathered green leaves, he sang a song in praise of his one true love. Suddenly Palamon leapt out of his hiding place and shouted fiercely. "Emily has only one true love and that is I, Palamon!"

The two men then flung themselves upon each other in a desperate rage. Palamon was like a raging lion and Arcite like a hungry tiger.

Heaven knows how the fight would have ended, but King Theseus came riding by with the queen, Princess Emily and his court. They found the two men now apart, out of breath.

"What's this? Who dares to fight in the royal forests?" King Theseus cried.

The two men were too angry to be careful, so they told the king their story.

"So you are Palamon and Arcite," said Theseus at last, "Palamon who has escaped from prison and Arcite who has unlawfully returned to my lands. I condemn you both to immediate death."

With tears in her eyes, Emily slipped off her horse and knelt in front of Theseus. "My Lord," she said, "I beg for the lives of these two young men. It is not their fault that they have been struck by cupid's arrow. I knew nothing of their love, but to kill them would be cruel."

The queen also pleaded with Theseus, and in the end he gave in. "Very well," he said to the two men. "Go back home, collect a hundred knights and return here. We will have a tournament, and the winner shall marry Princess Emily."

So Palamon and Arcite went away to call their friends together, and Emily sat in her high tower room, wondering which man she liked the best.

Theseus built a wonderful arena with stands, a jousting ring and three temples — one to Mars, the god of war, one to Venus, the goddess of love, and one to Diana, the goddess of young maidens.

Palamon and Arcite returned the night before the tournament, and each of them went to pray for success.

Arcite went to the temple of war. "Oh great god Mars," he prayed, "Give me victory in tomorrow's fight."

Palamon went to the temple of love. "Oh gentle goddess," he prayed, "let me win Princess Emily's heart."

Emily went to the temple of Diana. "If I am to marry, let it be to the one who will love me best."

The next day the tournament began. There was a great arranging of armour, fixing of spear-heads, buckling of helmets and polishing of shields. The trumpets sounded the charge. Out flew the swords, gleaming like polished silver. The fight was long and hard, but in the end Palamon was captured and Arcite was declared the winner. Full of excitement at his victory, he threw away his helmet and rode up the field to celebrate.

But the gods had planned so that all of the prayers might be answered. Arcite's horse stumbled and fell, throwing him heavily to the ground. He tragically died of his injuries, blessing Emily and begging Palamon's forgiveness with his last breath.

So Palamon won the fair Emily and long did they live in

bliss together. Emily loved Palamon tenderly, and he served her with so much gentleness that no word of anger was ever heard between them.

The Minstrel's Song

By Maud Lindsay

ONCE, LONG, LONG AGO, in a country over the sea there lived a prince called René, who married a lovely princess called Imogen.

Imogen came across the sea to the prince's beautiful country, and all his people welcomed her with great joy because the prince loved her.

"What can I do to please you today?"

the prince asked her every morning. One day the princess answered that she would like to hear all the minstrels in the prince's country, for they were said to be the finest in the world.

As soon as the prince heard this, he called his heralds and sent them throughout his land to sound their trumpets and call aloud, "Hear you minstrels! Prince René bids you come to play at his court on May Day, for love of the princess."

The minstrels were men who sang beautiful songs and played harps, and long ago they went about from place to place, from castle to castle, from palace to palace, and were always sure of a welcome wherever they roamed.

They could sing of the brave deeds of knights, and of wars and battles, and could tell of the mighty hunters who hunted in the great forests, and of fairies and goblins, better than a storybook. And because there were no storybooks in those days, everybody was glad to see them come.

So when the minstrels heard the prince's message, they hurried to the palace on May Day, and it so happened that some of them met on the way and decided to travel along together.

One of these minstrels was a young man named Harmonius. While the others talked of the songs they would sing, he gathered wildflowers from the roadside.

"I can sing of the drums and battles," said the oldest minstrel, whose hair was white and whose step was slow.

The Minstrel's Song

"I can sing of ladies and their fair faces," said the youngest minstrel, but Harmonius whispered, "Stop and listen! Listen!"

"We hear nothing at all but the wind in the tree-tops," said the others. "We have no time to stop."

They hurried on and left Harmonius. He stood under the trees and listened, for he heard something very sweet. At last he realized that it was the wind singing of its travels through the world, telling how it raced over the sea, tossing the waves and rocking the ships, and hurried on to the hills, where the trees made harps of their branches, and then how it blew down into the valleys, where all the flowers danced in time.

Harmonius listened until he

knew the whole song, and then he ran on to reach his friends, who were still talking of the incredible sights that they were to about to see.

"We shall see the prince and speak to him," said the oldest minstrel.

"And his golden crown and the princess's jewels," added the youngest. Harmonius had no chance to tell of the wind's song.

Now their path led them through the wood. As they talked, Harmonius said, "Hush! Listen!" But the others said, "Oh! That is only the sound of the brook trickling over the stones. Let us make haste to the prince's court."

But Harmonius stayed to hear the joyful song that the brook was singing, of its journey through mosses and ferns and shady ways, and of tumbling over the rocks in shining waterfalls on its long journey to the sea.

Harmonius sat and listened until he knew every word of the song off by heart, and then he hurried on to catch up with the others.

When he reached the others once more, they were still talking of the prince and princess, so he could not tell them of the brook. Then he heard something once again that was wonderfully sweet, and he cried, "Listen! Listen!"

"Oh! That is only a bird!" the others replied. "Let us make haste to the court, it is not far now."

But Harmonius would not go. The bird sang so joyfully that

Harmonius laughed when he heard its song. The bird was singing a song of green trees, and in every tree a nest, and in every nest some eggs! "Thank you, little bird," he said, "you have taught me a song." And he made haste to join his friends, for the palace was near.

When they arrived they were taken to see the prince and princess. The prince was thinking of the princess and the minstrels, but the princess was imagining her old home, and of the butterflies she had chased when she was a little child. One by one the minstrels played their harps before them. The oldest minstrel sang of battles and drums. The youngest minstrel sang of ladies and their fair faces, which pleased the court ladies very much.

Then came Harmonius. When he touched his harp and sang, the song sounded like the wind blowing, the sea roaring and the trees creaking. Then it grew very soft, and sounded like a trickling brook dripping on stones and running over little pebbles, and while the prince and princess and all the court listened in surprise, Harmonius's song grew ever sweeter. The princess shut her eyes as she listened to the music.

Then the prince came down from his throne to ask Harmonius if he came from fairyland with such a wonderful song. But Harmonius answered, "Three singers sang along the way, and I learnt the song from them today."

All the other minstrels looked up in

surprise when Harmonius spoke, and the oldest minstrel said, "We heard no music on our way."

But the princess said, "That is an old song. I heard it when I was a little child, and I can name the three singers." And so she did. Can you name them too?

Answer: The wind, the brook and the bird

How Princess Angelica Took a Little Maid

An extract from **The Rose and the Ring**
by William Makepeace Thackeray

One day, when Princess Angelica was still quite a little girl, she was walking in the garden of the palace with Mrs Gruffanuff, the governess. She was on her way to the royal pond to see the swans and ducks, and was carrying a bun to feed them.

How Princess Angelica Took a Little Maid

Angelica had not yet reached the duck pond, when a funny little girl came toddling up. She had a great quantity of hair blowing about her chubby little cheeks, and she looked as if she had not been washed for a long while.

The little girl wore a ragged bit of a cloak, and only one shoe.

"You little wretch, who on earth let you in here?" asked Mrs Gruffanuff angrily.

"Can I have dat bun?"

said the little girl, "me vely hungy."

"Hungry! What is that?" asked Princess Angelica, and she gave the child the bun.

"Oh, Princess!" said Mrs Gruffanuff, "How good, how truly angelical you are! See, Your Majesties," she said to the king and queen, who now came walking up to them, "how kind the princess is! She met this little wretch in the garden — I can't tell you why the guards did not stop her at the gate — and the dear princess has given her the whole of her bun!"

"But Mrs Gruffanuff, I didn't want it," said Angelica.

"You are a darling little angel all the same," said the governess.

"Yes, I know I am," said Angelica. "Dirty little girl, don't you think I am very pretty?"

Indeed, the princess had on the finest of little dresses, and, as her hair was carefully curled, she looked very pretty indeed.

"Oh, pooty, pooty!" said the little girl, laughing, dancing and munching her bun. As she ate it she began to sing, "Oh, what fun to have a plum bun! How I wis it never was done!" At which they all began to laugh merrily.

"I can dance as well as sing," said the little girl. "I can dance, and I can sing, and I can do all sorts of ting."

And she ran to a flowerbed, pulled out some flowers, made herself a little wreath, and danced before the king and queen so comically and prettily, that everybody was delighted.

"Who was your mother — who were your relations, little girl?" said the queen.

The little girl said, "Little lion was my brudder, great big lioness my mudder, neber heard of any udder."

So Angelica said to the queen, "My parrot flew away out of its cage yesterday, and I no longer care for any of my toys. I think this little dirty child will amuse me. I will take her home, and give her my old frocks…"

"Oh, the generous darling!" said Mrs Gruffanuff.

"…which I have worn ever so many times, and am quite tired of," Angelica went on, "and she shall be my maid. Will you come home with me, little girl?"

The child clapped her hands, and said, "Go home with you — yes!"

And they all laughed again, and took the child to the palace. The girl was given a

bath, and once washed and
combed she looked as
pretty as Angelica,

almost. Not that Angelica ever thought so,
for this little lady never imagined that
anybody in the world could be as pretty, as

good or as clever as her fine self.

In order that the little girl should not become too proud, Mrs Gruffanuff took her old ragged cloak and one shoe, and put them into a glass box. A card was then laid upon them, upon which was written,

These were the old clothes in which little Betsinda was found when the great goodness and admirable kindness of Her Royal Highness the Princess Angelica received this little outcast.

And the date was added, and the box locked up.

For a while little Betsinda was a great

favourite with the princess. She danced, sang, and made little rhymes to amuse her mistress. But then the princess got a monkey, and afterwards a little dog. After that she got a doll, and did not care for Betsinda any more. Betsinda became very quiet and sang no more funny songs, because nobody cared to hear her.

And then, as she grew older, she was made a little lady's maid to the princess, and though she had no wages, she worked hard and mended, and put Angelica's hair in papers, and was never cross when scolded, and was always eager to please. She was always up early and to bed late, and at hand when wanted, and in fact became a perfect little maid.

So the two girls grew up, and Betsinda was never tired of waiting on the princess.

She made her dresses better than the best dress-maker, and was useful in many ways.

Whilst the princess was having her lessons, Betsinda would watch, and in this way she picked up a great deal of learning – for she was always awake, though her mistress was not, and listened to the wise professors when Angelica was snoozing or thinking of the next ball.

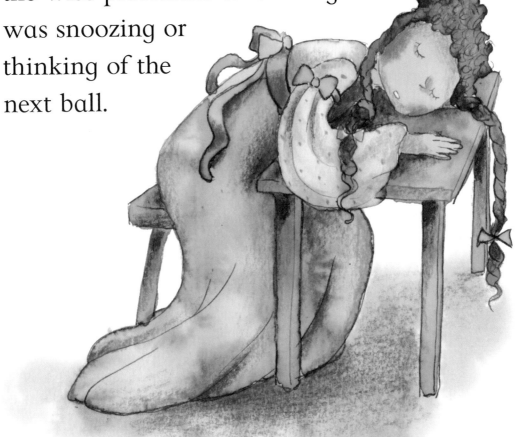

And when the dancing-master came, Betsinda learned along with Angelica, and when the music-master came, she watched him and practised the princess's pieces when Angelica was away at balls and parties. When the drawing-master came she took note of all he said and did — and the same with French, Italian and all the other languages.

When the princess was going out in the evening she would say, "Betsinda, you may as well finish what I have begun."

"Yes, miss," Betsinda would say, and sit down very cheerfully, not to FINISH what Angelica began, but to DO it.

For instance, the princess would begin to draw, let us say, a head of a warrior, but Betsinda would finish it. The princess would put her name to the drawing, and the court and king and queen would admire it, saying, "Was there ever a genius like Angelica?"

So, I am sorry to say, was it with the princess's embroidery and other accomplishments. Angelica actually believed that she did these things herself, and received all the flattery of the court as if every word of it was true. Thus she began to think that there was no young woman in all the world equal to herself, and that no young man was good enough for her. She had a very high opinion of herself indeed.

As for Betsinda, she heard none of these praises, so she was not puffed up by them, and being a most grateful, good-natured girl, she was only too anxious to do everything that might please her mistress.

So now you begin to perceive that

Angelica had faults of her own, and was by no means such a wonder of wonders as many people represented Her Royal Highness to be.

The Flower Princess

Anon

THERE WAS ONCE a princess so fair and lovely that the sun shone more brightly on her than on anyone else, the river stopped running when she walked by so that it might gaze on her beauty, and birds sang underneath her window at night.

Princes came to beg for her hand in marriage, but she swore she would only marry a prince who was kind, good and true. Many princes tried to convince her of their fine qualities, but none succeeded — until one day a prince from a small

kingdom came to woo her. He fell in love
with her, she could not resist him, and they
were married. She wore a silver
dress embroidered with crystal drops
and looked lovely. The court scattered
her path with rose petals and threw
sugar sweets as the couple walked past.
    But alas, trouble can come to all of us.

The prince's kingdom had an evil fairy. She was very beautiful but her beauty was spoilt by the cruelty and mean thoughts that she held inside.

When she saw the princess with her sweet, good face, her heart filled with jealousy and rage. She wove a spell to transform the princess into a flower in a nearby meadow.

The spell was not quite powerful enough to conquer the princess completely, so by night she appeared again in her true form, but every morning she had to transform into her flowery shape and spend the day in the meadow standing among the grasses and the other flowers.

One night she overheard the fairy talking and learnt how to break the spell. She told her husband, "If you come to the meadow

The Flower Princess

in the morning and pick me the
spell will be broken."
"How will I know
which one is you?" he said.
The princess did not know, for
her shape changed every day.
That morning she changed into a flower
and the prince hastened to the field to try
and find his love. He walked among the
grasses and the many flowers. How could
he find his love?
Then a thought came to him and he
looked closely at each bloom. Finally he
stopped before a blue cornflower, touched it
gently with his fingers, plucked it and
carried it back to his palace. As he passed
through the gates, the flower fell to the
ground and his princess stood before him.
"How did you find me?" she asked.

"Dew had fallen on all of the other flowers," he replied, "you alone had no dew upon you, for you had spent the night at the palace."